A Note to Parents

For many children, learning math is [hard. "I hate] math!" is their first response — to which many parents silently add "Me, too!" Children often see adults comfortably reading and writing, but they rarely have such models for mathematics. And math fear can be catching!

The easy-to-read stories in this **Hello Math Reader!** series were written to give children a positive introduction to mathematics and parents a pleasurable re-acquaintance with a subject that is important to everyone's life. **Hello Math Reader!** stories make mathematical ideas accessible, interesting, and fun for children. The activities and suggestions at the end of each book provide parents with a hands-on approach to help children develop mathematical interest and confidence.

Enjoy the mathematics!
• Give your child a chance to retell the story. The more familiar children are with the story, the more they will understand its mathematical concepts.
• Use the colorful illustrations to help children "hear and see" the math at work in the story.
• Treat the math activities as games to be played for fun. Follow your child's lead. Spend time on those activities that engage your child's interest and curiosity.
• Activities, especially ones using physical materials, help make abstract mathematical ideas concrete.

Learning is a messy process and learning about math calls for children to become immersed in lively experiences that help them make sense of mathematical concepts and symbols.

Although learning about numbers is basic to math, other ideas, such as identifying shapes and patterns, measuring, collecting and interpreting data, reasoning logically, and thinking about chance are also important. By reading these stories and having fun with the activities, you will help your child enthusiastically say "**Hello, math,**" instead of "I hate math."

—Marilyn Burns
National Mathematics Educator
Author of *The I Hate Mathematics! Book*

For Monica, Elly, Jim, and Margaret,
who know all the ways around "no."
— S.K.

For Patti Ann Harris
— J.S.

ISBN 0-439-05963-1

Copyright © 2001 by Scholastic Inc.
The activities on pages 27-32 copyright © 2001 by Marilyn Burns.
All rights reserved. Published by Scholastic Inc.
SCHOLASTIC, HELLO MATH READER, CARTWHEEL BOOKS and
associated logos are trademarks and/or registered trademarks of Scholastic Inc.

Library of Congress Cataloging-in-Publication Data

Keenan, Sheila.
    Lizzy's dizzy day / by Sheila Keenan ; illustrated by Jackie Snider ;
    math activities by Marilyn Burns.
       p.   cm. — (Hello math reader!. Level 2)
    Summary: Although she thinks she is helping with her cousin's birthday
party, Lizzy's mathematical reasoning does not always add up.
    [1. Problem solving — Fiction. 2. Mathematics — Fiction. 3. Parties — Fiction.
Stories in rhyme.] I. Snider, Jackie, ill. II. Burns, Marilyn. III. Title. IV. Series.
PZ8.3.K2295 Co 2001
[E] — dc21   00-029661

10 9 8 7 6 5 4 3 2 1   01 02 03 04 05 06

Printed in the U.S.A.   24
First printing, March 2001

Lizzy's Dizzy Day

by Sheila Keenan • Illustrated by Jackie Snider
Math Activities by Marilyn Burns

Hello Math Reader! — Level 2

Cartwheel
·B·O·O·K·S·®

SCHOLASTIC INC.
New York   Toronto   London   Auckland   Sydney
Mexico City   New Delhi   Hong Kong

Lizzy was the kind of girl
who liked to help out.
"Count me in," she'd say.
"Call on me. Give a shout."

Lizzy's cousin Finn lived
right next door.
Today was his birthday.
Finn was four.

"Do you need any help
with your party?" Lizzy said.
"Nope," said Finn
and shook his head.

But Lizzy never took "no" for
an answer.

Lizzy made a dozen cookies
and a really big mess.
Then she wrapped up her treat
and put on a dress.

She went over to Finn's.
He was leaving in a hurry.
"We're going to get my cake.
The door's open, don't worry."

Lizzy went inside
and put down her plate.
She looked at the table.
It was set for 8.

"I can give everyone a cookie
and still have more—
9, 10, 11, 12."
She ate the last 4.

Lizzy sat down and
made a face.
"Why is there a sock
hanging at each place?

"Now, *here* is something helpful
I can do."
Lizzy folded up the socks,
two by two.

Then she took the balloons
that were lying by each plate.
And blew them all up,
counting down from 8.

"8, 7, 6, 5, 4, 3, 2, 1. Done!"

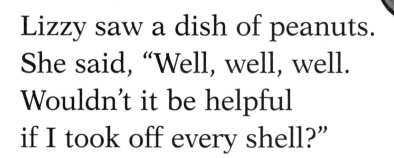

Lizzy saw a dish of peanuts.
She said, "Well, well, well.
Wouldn't it be helpful
if I took off every shell?"

So she counted all the nuts.
There were exactly 8.
By the time she finished shelling,
there were 5 left on the plate.

"1 lost, 7 shelled, 2 eaten. Yum!"

Next Lizzy saw
7 chairs in a line.
"Uh-oh," she said.
"This is not a good sign."

"There'll be 8 people at this party.
Where will we all sit?
This line needs another
chair in it."

Honk! Honk!

"Just in time," Lizzy said
and grinned a big grin.
"Surprise!" she yelled
when Finn walked in.

"You did need help here,"
Lizzy said.
Finn looked at her
and scratched his head.

Before Lizzy could tell Finn
anything more,
his 6 party friends
knocked at the door.

In came Jack, Jim, Bud, Tim,
Ted, and Nate.
With Finn and Lizzy,
that made 8.

Finn's mom said, "Okay, everyone,
find your place.
Let's have a blow-up-the-balloon race.

"Where are the balloons?"
Jack and Jim both said.
Lizzy's face turned
very red.

Finn's mom looked surprised.
But she said, "Never mind.
We can play a game
of another kind.

"See the sock hanging
on the back of your chair?
For the next game, that's what
you have to wear.

"Just pull that sock
right over your hand.
Then I'll blow bubbles.
Catch and pass them
before they land."

"Where are the socks?"
asked Tim and Ted.
Lizzy's ears burned
bright, bright red.

The peanut race was
also tough.
"Five nuts?" said Finn.
"That is not enough."

Nate chimed in,
"This game is swell,
but it's hard to push a peanut
without a shell."

Finn's mom told them all
how to play the next game.
Lizzy knew it wouldn't work —
and she was to blame.

But when the music started,
she got caught up in the race,
until the music stopped . . .

and everyone had a place!

Finn's mom said, "My! My!
What a surprise!
Well, since you're all seated,
you all get a prize."

"Whew!" said Lizzy.
"Now I know.
You can ask, 'May I help?'
But the answer could be 'no!'"

• ABOUT THE ACTIVITIES •

Learning to solve problems is one of the essential goals for children's math learning. To accomplish this, children need many experiences applying math concepts and skills to a variety of problem-solving situations. It's also important for children to see how math concepts and skills relate to real-world contexts.

Lizzy's Dizzy Day helps with both of these goals. In the story, Lizzy uses math to solve several numerical problems. However, Lizzy's solutions, while mathematically correct, create other problems unrelated either to the math ideas or the reasoning she used. Another important lesson when learning to solve problems in mathematics is that answers are only as valuable as they are sensible and appropriate for the situation at hand.

The activities that follow offer suggestions for revisiting the problems that Lizzy faced in the story and then extending them to give children further opportunities to think and reason numerically. Enjoy the activities, and have fun with math!

—Marilyn Burns

You'll find tips and suggestions
for guiding the activities whenever
you see a box like this!

Retelling the Story

How old was Lizzy's cousin Finn? How much older than Finn are you?

Lizzy baked a dozen cookies for Finn's party. How many cookies are there in 1 dozen?

When Lizzy went to Finn's house, she saw that the table was set for 8. She put a cookie at each place. How many cookies were left? What did Lizzy do with them?

There was 1 sock at each place. Lizzy folded all the socks into pairs. Now how many pairs of socks were there?

When Lizzy blew up the 8 balloons, she counted backwards. Can you count backwards from 8 down to 1?

Don't be surprised if counting backwards is difficult for your child. Knowing how to count doesn't necessarily translate into knowing the numbers in reverse order. (For example, you probably can't recite the alphabet backwards!) With practice counting backwards aloud, however, your child will improve. Start first with 3, then with 5, and then with larger numbers.

Next Lizzy took the shells off the 8 nuts in the dish. But she ate some, too. When she was finished, there were only 5 nuts in the dish. How many nuts did Lizzy eat?

Lizzy saw 7 chairs in a line. Why did she say that the line needed another chair?

When the party began, Finn's mom said, "Let's have a blow-up-the-balloon race." What was the problem?

Next Finn's mother told the children, "Pull that sock right over your hand." What was the problem? The peanut race was also tough. What was the problem there?

What game did the children play with the line of 8 chairs? What was the problem?

Lizzy had tried to help. What do you think she learned?

Sharing Cookies

Lizzy made 12 cookies. When she put them on 8 plates, there were 4 cookies left.

Suppose you were sharing the 12 cookies between just 2 people. How many would each person get? How many would be left over? Use 12 circles of paper as cookies and show how you could do this.

Then try sharing a dozen cookies for 3, 4, 5, 6, and 7 people. Use your paper cookies. How many are left each time?

Sharing a Dozen Cookies

Number of people	How many does each get?	How many are left over?
2		
3		
4		
5		
6		
7		
8	1	4

Sock Riddles

If Lizzy had only found 7 socks, she could only have made 3 pairs and there would be 1 sock left over!

Try these riddles. Each one tells how many socks you start with. You have to figure out if you will use them all up to make pairs or if you will have an extra sock left over.

You have 5 socks. Will you have 1 extra?
Hint: You can use pennies to check.

You have 6 socks.
You have 7 socks.
You have 10 socks.
You have 4 socks.
Will you have 1 extra?

Vary the numbers according to your child's comfort level. When numbers are hard for children, they tend to merely guess without figuring. When numbers are easy, they often blurt out the answer. Mix up the riddles with numbers that are hard and easy. Have pennies for your child to use to verify answers.

The Peanut Game

To play this game, you need your 2 hands, another person, and 8 peanuts. (You can also use pennies for the peanuts.)

After Lizzy ate some of the peanuts, there were 5 on the plate. Put 5 peanuts or pennies in one hand and hold it open. Put the rest of the peanuts or pennies in your other hand and make a fist to hide them. Now the other person guesses how many you are hiding. Then open your fist so you can both check.

Now try again. This time hide a different number of the 8 things in one fist and show the rest in your other hand. The other person guesses. Then open your hand so you can both check. Take turns so you have a chance to guess while the other person hides some peanuts or pennies.

More Peanut Games

Suppose there were only 7 peanuts to start? Or 10? Or more? Play the game for different numbers of peanuts or pennies. Count before you start each time so you both are sure how many there are all together.